21 days of
KINGDOM DECREES

CLYDE LEWIS

Lewis Ministries International
4936 NE Skidmore St
Portland, Oregon 97218

www.lewisministries.org

Ordering Information: Special discounts are available on bulk quantity purchases.

Contact: clyde@lewisministries.org.

Printed in the United States of America

INTRODUCTION

It's hard to keep a balanced spiritual life. Have you ever signed up for yearly/monthly/daily devotionals and daily scheduled prayer sessions only to fail at either of the two within a few weeks? Such lopsided spiritual growth is no way to mature as a believer.

I know, I have been there a couple of times. My mind would drift as I got distracted by never ending to-do lists. The truth remains that if both prayer and the word aren't a vital part of your day; you will never enjoy spiritual victory.

Studies have shown that close to 45% of Americans deal with this struggle every day. But this shall not be your case in Jesus' Name. You can have a balanced and effective spiritual life. You can have a vibrant devotional lifestyle. And you can do this with the simple technique of practicing what is in this book for less than 15 minutes every day.

It is said that it takes 21 days for a habit to form. In this book, I have prophetically prepared 21 days of powerful daily devotions paired with prophetic kingdom decrees. Prophetic decrees are powerful. The Bible records that we shall decree a thing and it shall come to pass (Job 22:28).

The world as we know it was formed at God's command. When He spoke, life came out of nothingness. The prophetic decrees that come from our mouths are powerful, forcible envoys that fulfill what the Lord has said in his word about us. In this book, you have an opportunity to set the tone for your day. By speaking the kingdom decrees at the end of each day's devotion out loudly with authority.

This is going to help you. It has done wonders in my life and others in my circle. I believe you will see tremendous changes in your life before it's over.

Perhaps you don't see the need to read this book today. If you don't, you run the risk of irreparably cementing a harmful habit of prayerlessness or not reading the word by missing out on the 21 daily devotionals and kingdom decrees.

So, what are you waiting for? A balanced and powerful spiritual life lies ahead of you. My advice to you, dear reader, is to keep reading, keep prophesying, and keep declaring. Don't stop and don't miss a single day.

TABLE OF CONTENTS

DAY 1

I SEIZE EVERYTHING THAT BELONGS TO ME.

From the moment John stepped onto the scene until now, the realm of heaven's kingdom is bursting forth, and passionate people have taken hold of its power.

Matthew 11:12 TPT

When we read this verse, most of us are left scratching our heads as to what Jesus was trying to say. Who are these men that take the kingdom of

God violently? The original word used there can be rightly translated to mean *"pressing forcefully."*

I firmly believe that the *"violence"* mentioned in today's verse is the distinguishing factor between those who are led by the spirit of God and those who aren't. Those who have tasted and encountered the God of the Bible are violent men and women. They carry a fierce enthusiasm for their Godly inheritance. They violently strive and push to enter the narrow gate.

You will not find them giving up easily after a few discouragements. No. They aren't careless beggars who move with the call of *"it is what it is."* They are awake and sober, and if God says something about them, they do not rest until they have laid hold of that promise.

Down on their knees, they go, again and again, crying out to God and warring with their prophecies. "Oh God, help me to lay hold of your promise. Help me with your grace." For the kingdom of heaven suffers violence and the violent take it by force.

Remember that the spoils of life are shared among the strong (Isaiah 53:12). Rise up, O sleeper, and take all that belongs to you. Be filled with holy violence.

DAY 1
KINGDOM DECREES.

- ❖ I decree and declare the blessing of God over all my plans and goals today.
- ❖ I declare that I am a violent man or woman who will walk into God's purpose for my life unrestricted.
- ❖ I declare that I am equipped with the right weapons for victory.
- ❖ I decree and declare that I am not a prisoner of circumstances.
- ❖ I decree and declare that angels are being released to fight on my behalf. That all my redemptive rights are restored in Jesus name.

DAY 2

GOD HAS A PLAN FOR ME.

"For I know the plans I have for you, declares the Lord, plans for welfare and not for evil, to give you a future and a hope."
Jeremiah 29:11 ESV.

The scripture, in many places, notes that our heavenly father has a specific plan for every one of us. Young Jeremiah couldn't bear the hate, reproach, and prejudice in Israel.

The king and the citizens nicknamed him the Prophet of Doom. And Jeremiah couldn't understand how this was God's plan for him. He gets a different response when he goes before the Lord, expecting a shoulder to cry on.

The Lord commands Jeremiah to walk shoulders up. To put down his sorrowful countenance with the reminder, "Before I formed you in the womb, I knew you; and before you were born, I consecrated you; I appointed you a prophet to the nations."

From the beginning of time, God's plan for every human being is that we should know him and receive his offer for our salvation. He is like a hopeless romantic, running after you and me. This is how much God loves us. There is no mountain he won't climb up, no wall he won't kick down while running after you.

Today, rest in the knowledge that God's plan is much bigger than you could ever imagine. His plan for you will lead you to your kingdom's destiny. Brethren, embrace it with hope and with joy.

DAY 2
KINGDOM DECREES

- ❖ I decree and declare that the plans that God has for me are here and now.
- ❖ I decree and declare that I will accomplish them with His divine protection.
- ❖ I decree that any enemy preventing me from achieving them is defeated in Jesus' Name.
- ❖ I decree and declare that today will be a great day.I walk shoulders up into what God has set for me.

DAY 3

I AM A NEW CREATION.

Now, if anyone is enfolded into Christ, he has become an entirely new person. All that is related to the old order has vanished. Behold, everything is fresh and new.
2 Corinthians 5:17 TPT.

We all look forward to New Year's Eve and the morning after. This is because it offers the opportunity for a fresh start. What Paul is telling the Corinthians is far better than starting over.

Think about a thief who has perfected the skill of robbery with violence. In the reality of their circumstances, it's unimaginable to think that such a person could be offered a fresh start. I mean, where would they hide, even if they repented?

What about the family that lost a member as a result of the actions of the thief? For such a person, it seems like there is no hope. It's almost laughable to dream that one day they can sleep and wake up with a brand new life. It sounds too good to be true.

This is the promise that Jesus has for all of us who have come to Him. He is not in the business of covering the past we have lived. Jesus doesn't nurse our prejudices. He kills them, washes us clean of all sin, and overhauls our lives. This happens as the Spirit of God takes up residence in our bodies. The only thing God requires of us is complete surrender.

And then the Holy Spirit, through the word of God, begins our moral education. The greatest miracle of all: a thief becomes a servant of God—a murderer like Saul becomes an Apostle. That, behold, for anyone who comes to Christ, old things have passed away.

Be reminded that God is in the business of transformation. He not only forgave, ransomed, and saved you, but He also made you a new creation.

DAY 3
KINGDOM DECREES.

- ❖ I decree and declare that I am not the same, for I have received new life, and my old ways are no more.
- ❖ I decree and declare that I am breaking family, generational, and personal barriers.
- ❖ I decree and declare that I am increasing on all sides.
- ❖ I decree and declare that I am blessed and forgiven.

DAY 4

I AM CONNECTED TO MY DESTINY

My dear brothers and sisters, what good is it if someone claims to have faith but demonstrates no good works to prove it? How could this kind of faith save anyone?
James 2:14 TPT

We have all struggled with faith—little or absence of it. When we look at the words of James, we are reminded of the essence of such faith. If we claim to have faith but lack its corresponding action, that faith is dead.

For this reason, the Bible teaches that faith is the only thing that pleases God and is the foundation of every believer's life. Our faith must be accompanied by evidential action to be alive.

This doesn't mean we won't face significant setbacks on our journey. But we must never allow any of these setbacks to limit the ability of God (Psalms 78:41). He has put within us the imagination to dream beyond any ceilings set on us.

Refuse to see yourself as a grasshopper anymore. (Numbers 13:33). See the new land and all it offers. Choose to see the deliverance of the Lord, and that shall be your testimony!

Let us believe the report of the Lord. Let us trust Him without seeing and hope without evidence. Spend time today asking God what limits you have put on yourself that have hindered your faith. Arise and shine, for your light has come!

DAY 4
KINGDOM DECREES

- ❖ I decree and declare that my faith is activated today.
- ❖ I decree and declare that my faith is moving mountains right now as I can step into my destiny.
- ❖ I decree and declare that I have an explosive faith that produces works.

DAY 5

I MOVE MOUNTAINS.

Jesus replied, "Let the faith of God be in you! Listen to the truth I speak to you: Whoever says to this mountain with great faith and does not doubt, 'Mountain, be lifted up and thrown into the midst of the sea,' and believes that what he says will happen, it will be done. **Mark 11:22-23 TPT**

The story of the fig tree was a lesson to point the disciples of Jesus to faith in God. Part of our ethos as believers is a lifestyle of prayer. We have private, corporate, written, intercessory, and many other prayers. In its simplest form, prayer can be described as having a conversation with God.

Unfortunately, there are some among us whose prayers are shaped by emotions. The feeling that we need to reach a certain level of "faith" before God can hear us. This falsehood springs with it two things. One is that when we pray, we must get our answer immediately, and two, if we don't get the results we anticipated, God doesn't hear our prayer.

Jesus tells the disciples to have faith *"in"* God. This is an essential prerequisite for moving mountains. We are off track whenever our faith insists only on prayer activities. You can fast for a year with zero results.

Faith in God is believing that He is bigger than all your problems. It is trusting Him to handle your mountains as He wishes and as it pleases Him.

The mountains in question are the immutable systems of this world. And God promises to move them on your behalf. Such faith recognizes the authority of God and knows for sure that there is nothing impossible for Him.

So, then pray in faith and without ceasing. Remember that God always answers prayers, even though the manifestation may not follow your expectations. Ask the Lord. Have no doubt, and He will give you your desires.

DAY 5
KINGDOM DECREES.

- ❖ I decree and declare that every mountain present in my life be relocated in Jesus name.
- ❖ I decree and declare that the mountains of poverty, discouragement, failure, abuse, and self-pity are trembling at the sound of my voice.
- ❖ I decree and declare that the manifestation of my prayers will be quickened in Jesus Name.
- ❖ I decree and declare that all my steps today will be ordered by the Lord.

DAY 6

JOY SHALL BE MY CONTINUAL FEAST.

Let joy be your continual feast. Make your life a prayer. And in the midst of everything be always giving thanks, for this is God's perfect plan for you in Christ Jesus.

1 Thessalonians 5:16 TPT

Many people have lost their joy in the daily transitions of life. I have not been spared either. However, I've also learned that when I draw from the presence of God, I receive fresh joy amidst every storm.

I love today's scripture, especially the part about letting joy be our continual feast no matter what we face in life. This is a truth to uphold whether we face marital issues, transition, financial issues, parental issues, career change, or any other season. Why? Because the joy that flows from the Father has no end.

I have personally experienced the joy of the Lord in the midst of unbelievable trials. I have found comfort in knowing that God always rejoices over me with dancing.

Chin up! It doesn't matter what storm you are battling today. Chin up! Feast on the joy of the Lord, and let it be your strength for the breakthrough coming your way.

DAY 6
KINGDOM DECREES

- ❖ Today, I decree and declare that I am feasting on the joy of the Lord.
- ❖ I decree and declare that every reason that brings pain is exterminated in the name of Jesus.
- ❖ I decree and declare that my life is experiencing the unusual joy of the Lord - it is springing up within me - Amen.

DAY 7

I AM NOT AFRAID.

This is my command—be strong and courageous! Do not be afraid or discouraged. For the Lord your God is with you wherever you go."
Joshua 1:9 NLT

Joshua had an arduous task. Moses, his spiritual mentor, had just died, and God had handed over the responsibility of leading Israel to him. He had served Moses for many years and knew the Israelites' character, weaknesses, and issues firsthand.

He was dealing with two challenges—that of the unknown future and that of rebellious Israelites. The journey ahead of the river Jordan was new. None of them had walked it again. Much discouragement came from the people themselves.

Similarly, in today's world, discouragement is all around us. People are preoccupied with what seems safe and orderly, not with what God has told us to do. How would you react if you were Joshua and you knew that your predecessor died out of disobedience, leading a rebellious people? All because he let the pressure of the crowd get to him.

We all have untamed situations in our lives, from sad little affairs to gloomy and dark ones. The one thing we must learn from Joshua is that fear is a choice. God's word is the only source of our courage.

There is a lesson here. The lesson that you must also learn. You can choose courage. Despite what you are going through and what you will face today, you can proclaim the word of God and believe it. Do not be afraid nor be dismayed.

DAY 7
KINGDOM DECREES.

- ❖ I decree and declare that I am free of all fear.
- ❖ I decree and declare that all the plans of the enemy over my life have come to naught.
- ❖ I decree and declare that God's perfect love for me dispels every discouragement thrown at me.
- ❖ I decree and declare that I am led by the Lord and empowered for every good work He gives me.

DAY 8

I WAS DESIGNED FOR PRAISE.

Let everything that breathes sing praises to the Lord! Praise the Lord!
Psalms 150:6 NLT.

You see, my friends, God designed us with one purpose only. The express purpose of praising Him. Psalms 150 is a clarion call for everything God created and gave life.

All that is around you right now—the insects, trees, animals, and humans—were created for praise. The winds worship Him, the mountains bow before him, and angels sing Hosanna to Him.

What happens when we praise? Many incidences of scripture confirm that praise is a weapon. Joshua praised, and Jericho's walls came down. Jehoshaphat raised praise, and God scattered Israel's enemies. As you lift your voice in praise, let all the challenges in your life die and scatter in the name of Jesus. I am excited to hear your testimonies.

David praised God for His mighty acts. If we sat down to count the blessings God has done for us one by one, the papers on this earth wouldn't be enough for a fraction of those deeds.

Look around you. What has the Lord done for you? Lift your voice in praise and name them one by one.

It's okay to take a pause. If you want to do a praise break in front of your mirror:
- Go ahead.
- Give Him thanks for all the victories He has brought your way.
- Praise Him for the joy that you have.

Take time to pray that God will take you into deeper levels of praise and worship.

DAY 8
KINGDOM DECREES

- ❖ I decree and declare that my praise brings down all the walls around me.
- ❖ I decree and declare I am about to experience a paradigm shift in my life.
- ❖ I decree and declare that God's presence is heavy around me all day long.
- ❖ I decree and declare that I am about to experience an abundance of breakthroughs.
- ❖ I decree and declare that as my praises go up, God's goodness and mercy is coming down on me like a shower.

DAY 9

I AM PROTECTED BY GOD.

He will rescue you from every hidden trap of the enemy, and he will protect you from false accusation and any deadly curse. His massive arms are wrapped around you, protecting you. You can run under his covering of majesty and hide. His arms of faithfulness are a shield keeping you from harm.
Psalms 91:3-4 TPT

Have you ever been in a situation where the circumstances required absolute courage despite what was happening? This happened to a young father in Colorado.

One day, while his five-year-old boy was playing outside, he heard loud screams. To the father's horror, he discovered that the boy was playing with a rather unexpected playmate; a mountain lion. The father mustered all the courage he could find and chased the cat standing on top of his child.

Such is a father's love. The father's heroic deeds remind God's steadfast and tenacious love for His children. In today's world, you only need to turn on your television to get a reason to be afraid: social injustices, pandemics, wars, and rumors of the same every minute of every day.

Psalms 91 describes these incidents as pestilence and snares. The enemy is on assignment to bring us down by all necessary means. But God has delivered us from all these traps. We must therefore remain girded under the protection of God.

Even when it feels like we have been pushed to the wall, we must remember the might of God's omnipotence. He promises to spread His wings over us and cover us. This is an image of a father's love.

God will deliver us from the terrors that come by night and day. It doesn't matter how dark the hour seems or how long you have been in the grave. God promises deliverance and protection.

DAY 9
KINGDOM DECREES

* ❖ I decree and declare that God, my father, loves me unconditionally.
* ❖ I decree and declare that God is my refuge and my fortress. No harm shall come to me or all that is called by my name.
* ❖ I decree and declare that my business/career/family is covered under the wings of Jesus.
* ❖ I decree and declare that I am delivered from the traps and snares of the enemy, including this (mention a current problem you are dealing with). I am victorious.

DAY 10

I AM WHO GOD SAYS I AM .

So fight with faith for the winner's prize! Lay your hands upon eternal life, to which you were called and about which you made the good confession before the multitude of witnesses!
1 Timothy 6:12 TPT.

Life is a battlefield. You are either a warrior or a loser. Our journey here on earth is essentially a war. This is a reality both for the saints and sinners. While for one is survival for the fittest, the other one is guaranteed a triumphant life.

This life doesn't give you what you deserve. It gives you what you demand of it. Failure to understand this truth will cost you and will make you wait for change until eternity.

When you receive Christ, you are born into the realm of warfare. The Bible says that whatever is born of God overcomes the world. You are born to conquer and confront the obstacles that come your way. You are born to overcome every circumstance in your life that is contrary to the truth of God's word.

Stop crying when you see obstacles. Stop shedding tears when challenges confront you. Fight! Warfare is a reality, but thankfully, your victory is also an eternal guarantee. So fight for the winner's prize. Don't stop until you have laid your hands on God's promise.

If you don't fight you will miss out on God's reward. Or even worse, you will live life as a victim of circumstance. God has promised to walk with you through every tribulation.

Child of God, don't cry as if God has lost His power. He is still in charge. And I guarantee that, if you trust Him, you will not only get through but also live a victorious life. So, fight on!

DAY 10
KINGDOM DECREES

- ❖ I decree and declare that I am a victor. I walk in the strength of God and the power of His might. I step boldly into the life God has called for me.
- ❖ I decree and declare that I am laying hold of God's promise over my life. My victory is guaranteed, and God has wiped all my tears away.
- ❖ I decree that I am superior to all the enemy's snares. Nothing can put me down.
- ❖ I declare that I am not ordinary. I live a supernatural life. Christ in me is an assurance of victory and glory over every circumstance I face.

DAY 11

I HEAR THE VOICE OF MY MASTER

My own sheep will hear my voice and I know each one, and they will follow me.
John 10:27 TPT

I can remember having a desire to learn to hear the voice of God early in my ministry. So many people around the world at that time were talking about hearing God's voice, and I felt left out. I wished I could understand what that looked like or how to do it.

For fear of embarrassment, I couldn't even ask my friends how they heard God's voice. Because I thought I should have already known the answer growing up a Christian. Therefore, I went on a personal quest to find the answers.

Unbeknownst to me, I was developing an intimate, loving relationship with the Holy Spirit. Then as I read books about God's voice and spent time praying, the Holy Spirit transformed my life right before me.

In John 10:27, Jesus declares to the disciples that His sheep hear His voice. You will learn that there are no secret steps, as I came to understand. We are the sheep, and Jesus is our shepherd. As you read today's devotion, I encourage you to just listen to the master's voice.

When you start listening, God's voice might sound like your own. But the Lord will give you the gift of discernment to distinguish it from other voices. Here is the key: God's voice brings peace, joy, and comfort, while the enemy's voice brings fear, impatience, and guilt.

My prayer for you is the same that Paul prayed over the church.

"I pray that the Father of glory, the God of our Lord Jesus Christ, would impart to you the riches of the Spirit of wisdom and the Spirit of revelation to know him through your deepening intimacy with him." (Ephesians 1:17 TPT)

DAY 11
KINGDOM DECREES

- ❖ I decree and declare that my ears are sensitive to hear the voice of my shepherd.
- ❖ I decree and declare that my intimacy with Jesus is deepening as I follow the voice of Jesus
- ❖ I decree and declare that I have the spirit of wisdom and revelation to know Jesus more
- ❖ I decree and declare that I am hearing the voice of God who called me by His grace, and I won't be afraid.

DAY 12

GOD HAS TURNED MY MOURNING INTO DANCING.

You have turned for me my mourning into dancing; you have loosed my sackcloth and clothed me with gladness, that my glory may sing your praise and not be silent. O Lord my God, I will give thanks to you forever! **Psalm 30:11-12 ESV**

The joy of humankind is fickle. It's as fragile as glass. During days of prosperity, praise and honor easily go to God. Contrariwise, life slips through our fingers during times of sorrow, and we drown in ruin and sadness.

The secret to a life of joy is identifying and aligning our lives with God in all seasons. How do you mourn the losses in your life? What do you do when you have worked in a company for decades only to get a retrenchment letter in your email?

Think of all the sorrows you have endured, betrayal by a friend, marital conflict, loneliness, losing a beloved, or receiving a negative medical report. At that time, what was going through your mind?

During such painful times of falling from prosperity to the pit, our only hope must be in the Lord. Only God can bring us up from the pit to praise. King David wrote the above psalm. He had faced his share of challenges by the time he wrote Psalms 30. David had discovered that he could only find confidence in God rather than living a life of what ifs and not.

God can turn all your mourning into dancing. Our God can take your anguish and your sorrow far away from you. He doesn't simply make them stop. He transforms it. Your sadness and tears are building blocks and "raw materials" in the hands of God. He takes your fear and failure and transforms them into gladness.

This is the promise that Paul reiterates when he says, " all things work together for good for those who love the Lord."

DAY 12
KINGDOM DECREES

❖ I decree and declare that every pain in my life is being transformed into gladness.
❖ I decree and declare that I do not grieve the way the world does. I grieve with hope and confidence.
❖ I decree and declare that all things work together for my good today in Jesus Name.
❖ I decree and declare that Jesus takes off every sackcloth of sadness and girds me with dancing.

DAY 13

THE JOY OF THE LORD IS MY STRENGTH.

Don't be dejected and sad, for the joy of the Lord is your strength!"
Nehemiah 8:10a, NLT.

Life is not always a smooth ride. Certain situations are ruthless and vicious, and they humble even pious believers. In such times where do we get our joy?

Who do we rely on when our resources have dwindled to naught? And yet there is no difficult hill that a believer faces that God can not handle.

The beautiful thing about walking with Jesus is that He becomes your joy daily. The smiles of those called by the Lord's name stem from God's storehouse of joy. It's a gift that pours and spills from heaven to all his children.

This is the joy Nehemiah 8 is reminding you about. That even in the middle of suffering, accidents, and heavy burdens of our current lives, God's joy will find a way to shine through. God's peace is so powerful that no one can explain it (Philippians 4:7).

Today, I decree this same joy over your life. Let it be your strength when life is bright and even when all seems dark.

DAY 13
KINGDOM DECREES

- ❖ I decree and declare an exceptional anointing of the joy of the Lord over my life.
- ❖ I decree and declare that nothing will take my joy away. I prophesy that depression, worry, and fear are departing my house in Jesus Name.
- ❖ I decree and declare that no matter how things look, I will keep my faith planted on the joy of the Lord, which is my strength.
- ❖ I decree and declare that my thirst and hunger for the joy of the Lord will be complete until I am overwhelmed with laughter and singing.

DAY 14

LIVING FROM A TRUE IDENTITY

But now, O Jacob, listen to the Lord who created you. O Israel, the one who formed you says, "Do not be afraid, for I have ransomed you. I have called you by name; you are mine.
Isaiah 43:1 NLT

Who am I? This is an important question we must all have personal answers to. There is such a phenomenon sweeping our world today called the identity crisis. If you don't know who you are, social media, news, friends, and society will try to define you using a template contrary to God's original script for your life.

For this reason, it's really easy to slip into the false identities that surround us. It's easy to pick up a label, a false identity to define ourselves, often as a way to feel like we belong to a particular group or trendy situation.

The thing is, when you become one with Christ, you are a new creation. (2 Corinthians 5:17). Those labels and identities shouldn't define you anymore. When you know who you are, you will know who you are not. You are a child of God (1 John 3:1). The life you now live, you live by faith in Jesus Christ.

If nothing else in your life is worth celebrating, find absolute rest in the description of your new identity—a new creation—a son or daughter. You're chosen and loved. You're more than enough. Start believing this truth today.

As you declare the following decrees, ask the Lord to show you more about your identity and who He has created you to be!

DAY 14
KINGDOM DECREES

❖ I declare I am a child of God and a new creation. I reign in life, career, and ministry.

❖ I decree and declare that I have power over sin. The life I live in the flesh, I live by faith.

❖ I declare that I am following the example of Jesus. He could have brought fire down from heaven, but he prayed for his persecutors.

❖ I decree and declare that I possess the fruit of self-control in all my daily dealings.

❖ I decree and declare that I will find favor and promotion because of my identity in Christ.

DAY 15

I WILL TRUST IN THE LORD.

Keep trusting in the Lord and do what is right in His eyes. Fix your heart on the promises of God and you will be secure, feasting on His faithfulness. Make God the utmost delight and pleasure of your life, and He will provide for you what you desire the most. Give God the right to direct your life, and as you trust Him along the way you'll find He pulled it off perfectly!

Psalm 37:3-5 TPT

I've been in many situations where life was throwing many curveballs at me, and I still had to trust God. And quite honestly, it was hard. Even when I prayed, sat, and listened to the Holy Spirit- He would usually say back to me, "Just trust me."

It's easy to say "you trust Him," but it's another thing to really submit to trust in Him. So how do you trust Him? By being obedient to the process and allowing Him to lead you. It's amazing when I trust Him through the process, and things work out.

I love what the Psalmist says in Psalms 37:3-5 about trusting in the Lord and keeping our eyes focused on Him. We usually find that when we keep our eyes focused on Him, our heart shifts as we see the promises of God come through. The other part I love about the Psalms is that if we truly delight in the Word, He can bring things that He promised us to pass. *"Delight"* in Hebrew means to be soft or tender.

Just those words, *"soft or tender,"* are so powerful because God wants us to be tender in a pliable way to whatever we are going through. When we remember to delight in Him, He gives us our heart's true desires.

However, to get the desires of our hearts, we must be softened. This is connected to our faith and trust in Him that He will do what He has promised.

I love verse 5 more because it talks about us giving everything over to God to let Him order our steps. Once again, it goes back to trusting Him to order those steps and not us placing trust in ourselves. God can pull it off perfectly, where we cannot.

Whatever you are facing at this moment- know that God will bring you through, but it all starts with you trusting and delighting in Him. Let your heart be so softened that He can fulfill your heart's desire. He is not a God that fails. He is a God that believes in you, and God thinks you can do anything!

DAY 15

KINGDOM DECREES

- ❖ I decree and declare that God would give me the desires of my heart.
- ❖ I decree and declare that no weapon formed against me shall prosper and I shall be obedient to the will of the Father.
- ❖ I decree and declare that I will keep my eyes focused on the Father and He will make my path straight.

DAY 16

PEACE IN THE MIDST OF A STORM.

But Jesus reprimanded them. "Why are you gripped with fear? Where is your faith?" Then he stood and rebuked the storm, saying, "Be still!" And instantly it became perfectly calm.
Matthew 8:26 TPT

You have probably heard about the story of Jesus and the disciples in the boat before. There are certain parallels we can draw from the story to our own lives.

The storm came out of nowhere, threatened to sink the boat, and caused much fear among the disciples. Funny enough, Jesus was sound asleep, unafraid, and unscathed by the whole situation. When they called out to Him, it was out of despair.

They had probably tried everything else and failed. Remember that a majority of the disciples were fishermen. This wouldn't have been their first rodeo in the tough Galilean waters.

However, this case was a little different. The waves were harder, and the winds were more unforgiving. Jesus, probably still wiping his eyes, woke up to see them terrified. He lifted His hand and commanded the sea to be still, and it obeyed.

Many of the issues we face and endure in life appear out of nowhere, like this storm. We all know that one day we will have to survive a storm, but nobody knows when it will show up. When this happens, and trouble is beating at the boat of our lives, let us choose to trust Jesus to calm the storm and not our own devices.

Some of us might be going through a challenging period today as we talk about this. Maybe you feel scared, threatened, and unaware of how to proceed forward. And you say, "Does the Lord really love me when the wicked around me seem to prosper?" (Psalms 73).

I have good news for you. You must not doubt it. Fix your eyes on Jesus. He is in the boat with you. Find him, and you will find peace.

DAY 16
KINGDOM DECREES.

- ❖ I decree and declare protection from all unseen dangers.
- ❖ I decree and declare that every storm and wind of the enemy sent against my life is failing now, in the name of Jesus.
- ❖ I prophesy to my future. It will be a year of peace, calmness, victory, breakthroughs, and impossible miracles.

DAY 17

I AM LOVED WITH AN EVERLASTING LOVE

The Lord appeared to him from far away. I have loved you with an everlasting love; therefore, I have continued my faithfulness to you. **Jeremiah 31:3 ESV**

Love is a beautiful thing. J. Allan Petersen told the story of a newspaper columnist who handled a wife with so much hatred for her husband. When the columnist saw how hell-bent she was on divorce, he proposed a solution for the lady.

"Return home and pretend to love your husband. Take care of him and give him praise for all his virtues. Try to be as considerate, kind, and generous as possible. Make an effort to make him happy and have fun with him."

Convince him of your unwavering love and inability to survive away from his presence. Once this has happened for some time, drop the bomb. Let him know that you want to get a divorce. He will suffer a great deal as a result of that. "

With excitement and enthusiasm, the lady couldn't hold back her grin. She smiled ear to ear, not forgetting to thank the columnist for such a wonderful idea for revenge. Two months into her act, the columnist was worried that he hadn't heard from her. When he reached out, he got the answer he was expecting. She said, " I cannot divorce my husband. I discovered how much I loved him. "

Love is an action, a sacrificial action. When it's mentioned outside those boundaries, it is fake. In Jeremiah 31:3, God unequivocally says to Israel, "I have loved you." Think about it. God was professing love to a people whose lives were characterized by rebelliousness.

In the same way, he is still professing that love to us today. Despite our rebellion and backsliding, God looks down from His throne in heaven and declares, "I love you with an everlasting love." What could be sweeter than this? It's not just any love. It's a declaration of an endless never-failing eternal love. God loves you forever and ever.

DAY 17
KINGDOM DECREES

- ❖ I decree and declare that I am a partaker of God's limitless love.
- ❖ I decree and declare that all other voices contrary to God's love in my life go silent now in the name of Jesus.
- ❖ I decree and declare that God's love is changing me on the inside out.
- ❖ I decree and declare that God's opinion of me is valid. He is delighted with my life, and that truth is my strength.

DAY 18

I AM WINNING EVERYDAY

No, in all these things we are more than conquerors through him who loved us.
Romans 8:37 ESV

When God speaks about us, He speaks as if it were already so. And after hearing His words, many of us wonder if God even knows the person He is talking about.

When we look at ourselves, we only see our frailty, disadvantages, and weaknesses—not our strengths, advantages, or future glory. But God doesn't look at the things men look at. Men look at the outward appearance, but God looks at the heart (1 Samuel 16:7).

In Judges 6, God called Gideon a mighty man of valor when He found him hiding from the Philistines. And later, through faith, Gideon put the armies of the enemy to flight, subdued kingdoms, and obtained the promise of God for Israel.

Today, God calls you *more than a conqueror* through the one who loves us, irrespective of what is happening in your life.

Because if you have Jesus in your life, you have dominion over all things. Dominion over sickness, sin, pain, and every disadvantage life throws at you. This means living a life of zero defeats, zero setbacks, and winning every day. This is the life that God sees in you.

Victory is not your ambition. It is your heritage. Take it up by faith in the word of God. Believe it, and you will never be at a disadvantage.

DAY 18
KINGDOM DECREES

* ❖ I decree and declare that I have Jesus in my life. I am on fire every day, and nothing can stop me. No matter what I face, I win every day.
* ❖ I decree and declare that I have overcome the world. I am eternally victorious. I am free of every incurable illness, and I am living in the perfect will of God.
* ❖ I decree and declare that I am who God says I am. I am more than a conqueror because the glory of God is revealed in me, and the greater one lives in me.
* ❖ I decree and declare that my life is a blessing. Every impossible need in my life is fulfilled, and God is doing big things for me and through me in the name of Jesus Christ.

DAY 19

MY LIFE IS DIVINELY FAVORED.

And we know that for those who love God all things work together for good, for those who are called according to his purpose.
Romans 8:28 ESV

We all face things that we don't understand in our lives. Things that take longer than expected. Doors that remain closed and betrayal from friends. At such times, it is easy to be frustrated and wonder whether God has abandoned us.

Psalms 119:91 says that all things work together to serve the plan of God. When good things happen, we can see how they serve the good purposes of God. But when bad things happen, it's a different story. What we don't realize, though, is that even the negative things happen to serve God's purpose.

The lost contract and the person who walked away from you are serving God's plan. Perhaps you are in a silent season of doing the right thing but seeing no growth, and you wonder how this serves God. Or you were up for promotion, and your boss gave it to a person with lesser experience than you. Beloved, take heart. This, too, will work together for your good.

Jesus endured hardship, hate, and even betrayal from one of the twelve disciples he had chosen. Had He not gone through such betrayal, we wouldn't have salvation today through His death and resurrection. Through the testimony of Jesus, we should see difficulties in a new light. Perhaps without that season of hardship, you wouldn't be prepared for what God has in store for you in the future.

No distinguished person has ever reached their destiny without opposition. It might be uncomfortable, but God wouldn't have allowed it if it was not meant to work for your good.

Perhaps you are in debt, and there is no help in sight. Keep your faith alive. You will settle the creditors. Maybe you have been betrayed, and your heart is broken. Wipe your tears. Give thanks for all the things happening in your life.

Child of God, nothing can override the purposes of God for your life. Embrace the detours and the painful seasons because God is using them to move you into your purpose. All will be well!

DAY 19
KINGDOM DECREES

- ❖ I decree and declare that I maintain prevailing faith even when I am troubled from all sides or in the roughest storms of life.
- ❖ I decree and declare that no matter what I face, everything is working together for my good, according to God's word.

❖ I decree that I have everything God says I have. Nothing will separate me from God's love, persecuted but not forsaken. "Casted down but not destroyed."

❖ I decree and declare that I am flourishing and prevailing over hardships like the cedars of Lebanon. I am divinely favored. Glory to God!

DAY 20

GOD DELIGHTS IN MY PRAYERS.

And this is the confidence that we have toward him, that if we ask anything according to his will, he hears us. And if we know that he hears us in whatever we ask, we know that we have the requests that we have asked of him.
1 John 5:14-15 ESV

"Oh, that every Christian enterprise commenced with prayer, continued with prayer, and crowned with prayer! Then we might also expect to see it crowned with God's blessing.— Charles Spurgeon.

Have you ever wondered what it takes to have a prevailing prayer life? To have answers for the prayers you make.

It takes confident faith. Look at the men in the bible who were able to obtain something from God. Their faith was bold. Blind Bartimaeus shouted loudly for Jesus while those around him tried to shut him up.

I put it to you that laying hold of your breakthrough only requires the ingredient of boldness. It is this confident faith that brought the prodigal son home. It is this faith that caused prophet Elijah to humiliate 450 false prophets of Baal, for a whole afternoon.

So let us come boldly to the throne of our gracious God. There we will receive his mercy, and we will find grace to help us when we need it most. (Hebrews 4:16). This is the confidence that John was writing about.

Therefore prayer is neither beggarly nor pride. Prayer is children coming boldly to their father for whatever they need.

Today be bold and you will get raw answers for your prayers. Be bold and God will hear when you call upon his name. God delights in your prayers.

DAY 20
KINGDOM DECREES

- ❖ Lord, I am thankful for the opportunity to pray. Thank you for delighting in my prayers.
- ❖ I decree and declare that my prayers are effective and they avail much power to effect the will of God on earth.
- ❖ I decree and declare that I am released from the spirit of smallness and doubt. I am a partner with God to exercise His dominion over cohorts of darkness, Satan and circumstances.
- ❖ I decree and declare that I am confident of God's power in me.

DAY 21

ANYTHING IS POSSIBLE.

Looking into their eyes, Jesus replied, "Humanly speaking, no one, because no one can save himself. But what seems impossible to you is never impossible to God!"
Matthew 19:26 TPT

Jesus loves to exceed our expectations. He doesn't just answer our prayers. Jesus answers *exceedingly abundantly above all we can ever ask or imagine*. He goes the extra mile.

When the prodigal son was going back home, his heart was only set on repenting. He expected to have a nice cool talk with the father. Instead, the father received him with a big feast that necessitated inviting the neighbors (Luke 15).

You might be fixated on what is happening in your life today. But God sees your eternal destiny. We miss out on this promise when we walk according to our feelings. If God can create the whole world from nothing, what can he not do with your life?

To be spiritual is to know that there are no impossibilities with God. *With* God, *all* things are possible. Our only prerequisite is to partner with Him through faith. Mark 9:23 says that if only we can believe, all things are possible. The one who believes can do anything, be anything and achieve anything.

So you must ask yourself what it is that you believe. Do you believe that your children can change and come back home? Do you believe you can walk again? Do you believe that you can see or hear again?

Stop crying, child of God. There is no sickness God cannot heal. There is no mountain He cannot move. Nothing is too hard for Him. He raised Lazarus after three days. Whatever you shall believe of the Lord, that you shall receive.

Don't look at the famine ravaging your life. It makes no difference what might be ahead of you, behind you, or around you, for nothing shall be impossible for you (Matt 17:20). Trust God. Hand over the issue to Him. He is more passionate about your success than you could be.

DAY 21
KINGDOM DECREES

- ❖ I decree and declare that there is nothing too hard for my God to do and that every hard situation in my life is solved today.
- ❖ I decree and declare that all dead things in my life are coming back to life. After today, what seemed impossible will be a testimony.
- ❖ I decree and declare that every mountain of impossibility standing in my way is melting like wax. My path is shining brighter and brighter until the perfect day.
- ❖ I decree and declare that nothing is impossible in my life. I walk in endless victory and possibilities.

BONUS DAY

GOD HAS ALREADY MADE A WAY

I am the Lord, your Holy One, the Creator of Israel, your King." Thus, says the Lord, who makes a way in the sea, a path in the mighty waters,
Isaiah 43:15-16 ESV

David was running from the man who he had protected and served. He was running from an army he probably had trained. He served at the palace in one season, and in the other, he hid in caves.

We have all had times and seasons where we couldn't think of escape. At such a period, it's not easy to be full of confidence and hope in God. And yet, God expects us to leave all that fear and nervousness behind us. He expects us to trust His ability to make a way in the wilderness.

God is rarely predictable, but He is always faithful. Even when all the walls seem to be closing together and you are in the toughest of situations, He still has it all figured out. His power shines the brightest in seemingly hopeless situations.

Because of His love toward you, He will move mountains, close the mouths of lions, open prison doors and conquer any giant to bring victory your way.

Child of God, whatever might be troubling at present, give it to Him. Philippians 4:6 says we should not be pulled in different directions worrying about anything. Instead, we should be saturated in prayer daily, offering our faith-filled requests before

God with overflowing gratitude. (Philippians 4:6, TPT).

We are in a season of trouble. Gas prices are rising. So much is changing overnight. Have faith in God for food. He will not only make way for you to get a job in that company, but he can also make you the owner. Sounds impossible? Remember, it took only one night for Joseph to move from being a prisoner to a prime minister with a wife and prime land in Egypt.

It might sound crazy, but God will bring you out of your situation. He will make way for you out of your trouble. What God has for you will shock you. All you have to do is believe it.

BONUS DAY
KINGDOM DECREES

❖ I decree and declare that today is a day full of open doors. Thank you Lord for providing all that I require for life and godliness.
❖ I decree and declare that as I am programmed for greatness. I am encouraged, empowered and motivated to reach my destiny.

❖ I decree and declare that because God is ahead of me, all the mountains in my life are leveled. All the bronze gates are falling and God is giving me riches stored in secret places.

❖ I decree and declare that gates are bowing down before me and doors shut against my prosperity are opening up by fire in Jesus Name.

ABOUT THE AUTHOR

Clyde Lewis is an author, speaker, church planter, and pastor of Destiny Church International in Portland, Oregon. He is currently planting four new churches across the US, as well as serving globally as the apostolic prophet at Lewis Ministries International.

In addition, Clyde is the CEO of Rebuild Your Identity Leadership, providing executive coaching to clients in corporate America as well as 1:1 and group coaching to inspire entrepreneurs and leaders at all levels. He is passionate about helping people rediscover their identity and love their life!

Clyde is also certified to coach kingdom builders using many different tools, including: Kolbe Certified

Consultant, John C. Maxwell Certified Coach, Dave Ramsey Financial Coach, Life Language Communication Coach, Enneagram Coaching, and many more.

A few of his other accomplishments include:
- Ordained Apostle/Prophet through Christian International
- Founder of the School of the Prophet
- Head Chaplain for the Portland Police Bureau
- Certified Anger Management Consultant
- President of Lighthouse Bible Institution
- Clyde lives in Portland Oregon with his wonderful wife Lisa and their two beautiful children.